Angelina Ba
Family Fun Day

Based on the story by Katharine Holabird
Based on the illustrations by Helen Craig

SIMON SPOTLIGHT
An imprint of Simon and Schuster Children's Publishing Division
New York London Toronto Sydney New Delhi
1230 Avenue of the Americas, New York, New York 10020 • This Simon Spotlight paperback edition August 2021 • Illustrations by Mike Deas
© 2021 Helen Craig Ltd. and Katharine Holabird. The Angelina Ballerina name and character and the dancing Angelina logo are trademarks of HIT
Entertainment Limited, Katharine Holabird, and Helen Craig. All rights reserved, including the right of reproduction in whole or in part in any form.
SIMON SPOTLIGHT and colophon are registered trademarks of Simon & Schuster, Inc.
For information about special discounts for bulk purchases, please contact Simon & Schuster Special Sales
at 1-866-506-1949 or business@simonandschuster.com • Manufactured in the United States of America 0721 LAK
10 9 8 7 6 5 4 3 2 1 • ISBN 978-1-5344-9562-3 (pbk) • ISBN 978-1-5344-9563-0 (ebook)

It was a beautiful sunny day in Chipping Cheddar. Angelina Ballerina was having breakfast with her family. Mr. Mouseling had made his famous cheddar waffles!

"What a lovely day," said Mr. Mouseling. "Let's go to the park."

"Please, can we have a picnic?" asked Angelina.

"That is a wonderful idea," Mrs. Mouseling agreed. "Would you and your sister like to help pack the picnic basket?"

Angelina's little sister, Polly, jumped up and down with excitement.

"We'd love to!" said Angelina.

"I'll bring our kites," said Mr. Mouseling.

When they got to the park, Angelina and Polly carefully laid out the picnic. There were delicious cheddar muffins, fruit salad, and a cheeseberry pie for dessert.

"Yummy!" said Polly.

After lunch the two sisters snuggled together, and Angelina read a story to Polly.

As soon as Angelina finished reading, she had an idea. "The wind is blowing. Let's fly our kites!" she said.

Oh no! Polly's kite kept getting stuck in the trees!
"Don't worry, I'll help you," said Angelina kindly.

Afterwards, Angelina had another idea. "Let's do ballet outdoors!" she said.

Angelina twirled around the meadow and performed pliés and curtsies.

Polly tried to be graceful like Angelina, but she wiggled and wobbled as she twirled behind her big sister.

"Good practice, Polly!" said Angelina. "Now let's go for a ride on the seesaw!"

The two mouselings raced to the seesaw. It was fun at first, but Polly was always up in the air because she was smaller.

"I know! Let's go to the carousel," Angelina suggested.

They rushed to the carousel, but sadly Polly wasn't tall enough to go on the ride.

Polly walked away and started to cry.

Angelina was very sorry for her little sister. Polly wasn't having much fun at all!

Then Angelina had another idea. "There are still fun things we can do. Let's play tag! You're it!"

Polly loved to play tag, but she couldn't run as fast as Angelina.

Angelina slowed down and made sure Polly could tag her. That made Polly very happy!

After tag the two sisters got the giggles and fell in a heap on the grass.

Then they heard the ice cream truck, and they both jumped up to get an ice cream. Angelina asked for a cup of chocolate ice cream, and Polly asked for a vanilla cone. As they skipped happily back through the park, Polly dropped her cone. Oh no!

"Here, Polly," said Angelina, offering her ice cream. "You can hare mine."

"Oooh, thank you, Angelina!" said Polly.

Angelina put her arm around her sister.

"I will always share my ice cream with you," she promised.

As the sun began to set, Angelina and her family packed up their picnic and walked home. "I had a really nice family fun day!" Angelina said.

Polly giggled. "Me too!" she said.